Withdrawn

Exploring World Cultures

Belgium

By Rachael Morlock

Cavendish
Square

New York

Published in 2022 by Cavendish Square Publishing, LLC
243 5th Avenue, Suite 136, New York, NY 10016

Website: cavendishsq.com

This publication represents the opinions and views of the author based on his or her personal experience, knowledge, and research. The information in this book serves as a general guide only. The author and publisher have used their best efforts in preparing this book and disclaim liability rising directly or indirectly from the use and application of this book.

All websites were available and accurate when this book was sent to press.

Library of Congress Cataloging-in-Publication Data

Names: Morlock, Rachael, author.
Title: Belgium / Rachael Morlock.
Description: First Edition. | New York : Cavendish Square Publishing, 2022.
| Series: Exploring world cultures | Includes index.
Identifiers: LCCN 2020040961 | ISBN 9781502658883 (Library Binding) | ISBN
9781502658869 (Paperback) | ISBN 9781502658876 (Set) | ISBN
9781502658890 (eBook)
Subjects: LCSH: Belgium--Juvenile literature. | Belgium--Description and
travel. | Belgium--History--Juvenile literature. | Belgium--Social life
and customs.
Classification: LCC DH418 .M66 2022 | DDC 949.3--dc23
LC record available at https://lccn.loc.gov/2020040961

Editor: Katie Kawa
Copy Editor: Nicole Horning
Designer: Jessica Nevins

The photographs in this book are used by permission and through the courtesy of: Cover CroMary/Shutterstock.com; p. 4 Melissa Alvarez/EyeEm/Getty Images; p. 5 Westend61/Getty Images; p. 6 PeterHermesFurian/iStock/Getty Images Plus; p. 7 George Pachantouris/Moment/Getty Images; p. 8 Fine Art Images/Heritage Images/Getty Images; p. 9 Godong/Stone/Getty Images; p. 10 WEKWEK/E+/Getty Images; p. 11 Photonews/Getty Images; pp. 12, 29 Jon Hicks/Stone/Getty Images; p. 13 Peter Dazeley/The Image Bank/Getty Images; p. 14 EMMANUEL DUNAND/AFP via Getty Images; p. 15 Romy Arroyo Fernandez/NurPhoto via Getty Images; p. 16 Choong Jackie/EyeEm/Getty Images; p. 17 Bryngelzon/E+/Getty Images; p. 18 In Pictures Ltd./Corbis via Getty Images; p. 19 Vincent Kalut/Photonews via Getty Images; p. 20 Alexander Sorokopud/Moment Unreleased/Getty Images; p. 21 Jonathan Raa/NurPhoto via Getty Images; p. 22 DOMINIQUE FAGET/AFP via Getty Images; pp. 23, 25 Mark Renders/Getty Images; p. 24 Olivier Matthys/Getty Images; p. 26 Arterra/Universal Images Group via Getty Images; p. 27 Tim de Waele/Getty Images; p. 28 stevenallan/E+/Getty Images.

Some of the images in this book illustrate individuals who are models. The depictions do not imply actual situations or events.

CPSIA compliance information: Batch #CS22CSQ: For further information contact Cavendish Square Publishing LLC, New York, New York, at 1-877-980-4450.

Printed in the United States of America

Find us on

Contents

The Kingdom of Belgium is known around the world for its fine chocolates, colorful parades, beautiful lace, comic strips, waffles, and more. Visitors to Belgium will find the sleek,

Belgian waffles are popular around the world!

modern headquarters of world **organizations** alongside old, stone castles and churches. It's hard to believe so many cool things can be found in such a small area!

Belgium is one of Europe's smallest countries. It's about the size of Maryland in the United States. Still, it's played a large part in European history and life in Europe today. Belgium is also home to many people. There were more than 11 million people living there in 2020.

Shown here is Brussels, which is the capital of Belgium.

Many larger countries and empires—groups of land and people under one ruler—claimed Belgium as their own throughout history. Then, Belgium declared, or called, itself an independent country in 1830. World wars and fighting among groups within Belgium have shaken the country at times. However, Belgium has kept growing. Its special character and culture, or way of life, are still strong.

The northwestern part of Belgium touches the North Sea. Elsewhere, Belgium is surrounded by the Netherlands, Germany, Luxembourg, and France. Altogether,

This map of Belgium shows its neighboring countries and its major cities.

Belgium's area covers 11,787 square miles (30,528 square kilometers).

Most of the land in the north is low and flat. Hills roll along the middle of the country. Taller peaks rise out of the Ardennes region, or area,

FACT!

Botrange—a peak in the Ardennes—is Belgium's highest point at 2,277 feet (694 meters).

in the south. Rivers and **canals** flow across the country. The Scheldt (or Schelde) and the Meuse are two main rivers in Belgium.

The Ardennes region is sometimes known as the Ardennes Forest because of how many trees cover the land.

Belgium has regular rain, clouds, and fog. It has warm summers and cool winters. Strong winds often blow in from the North Sea and quickly change the weather. Belgium's coast and rivers sometimes flood.

Belgian Wildlife

Wild boars, deer, and wildcats live in the Ardennes region of Belgium. Birds such as sandpipers and snipes live in the lowlands. Belgium is also home to wild hamsters!

The word "Belgium" comes from the ancient Roman name for the people who lived in what's now Belgium. These people were ruled by the Romans. In later centuries, the Dukes of Burgundy and rulers from

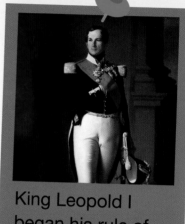

King Leopold I began his rule of Belgium in 1831.

Spain, Austria, France, and the Netherlands all had turns controlling this land.

Belgium joined the United Kingdom of the Netherlands in 1815. However, many Belgians disagreed with the Dutch king about important

FACT!

Leopold I was the first king of independent Belgium.

8

The Battle of Waterloo

Napoleon Bonaparte, who was a French emperor, was famously beaten at the Battle of Waterloo in Belgium in 1815. This battle marked the end of Napoleon's period of rule over much of Europe.

issues. A **revolution** that began in 1830 led to Belgium's independence.

New problems came up when the Germans **invaded** the country during World War I (1914–1918) and World War II (1939–1945). In addition, differences based on culture and religion, or a person's belief system, have tested Belgium's strength throughout history.

These gravestones honor fallen soldiers from World War I. Important battles in World War I and World War II were fought in Belgium.

Belgium is a constitutional monarchy. This means it has a king or queen, but their power is limited by a constitution—a document that sets up a country's laws and government.

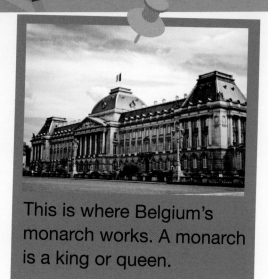

This is where Belgium's monarch works. A monarch is a king or queen.

Belgium's branches of government are explained in its constitution. The monarch heads the executive branch. Parliament makes laws in the legislative branch. The courts make up the judicial branch. A prime minister is chosen

FACT!

Belgium's parliament is divided into a Senate and Chamber of Representatives.

Levels of Government

Regional governments in Belgium make decisions about farming, the natural world, and how people get from place to place. Language communities have power over schooling and things dealing with culture.

by the monarch and allowed by parliament to be the head of the government.

Today, Belgium is broken up into three regions. Flanders is a Flemish-speaking region in the north. The French-speaking

Sophie Wilmès became Belgium's first female prime minister in 2019.

region in the south is called Wallonia. The Brussels-Capital region is in the center of the country. Belgium also has three language communities: French, Flemish, and German.

Belgium's **resources** and location have built up its economy, or its system of making, buying, and selling goods and services. Belgium has been a major hub for European trade

Handcrafted lace has always been an important part of Belgium's textile trade.

throughout history. In the past, its textile trade was very important. Textiles are a type of cloth. Coal mines also helped Belgium build wealth.

Now, natural resources such as sand for making glass, chalk and limestone for

Belgium is part of a partnership of European countries called the European Union (EU).

A Shining Trade

Antwerp is the second-largest seaport in Europe. Important goods pass through this Belgian port, including 80 percent of the world's rough diamonds.

construction, and clay for pottery help keep the Belgian economy steady. Workers also make cars, metals, chemicals, and food. Most Belgians

Like other members of the EU, Belgium's currency, or money, is the euro.

have service jobs. They're based in health care, government, banking, and **tourism**.

Belgian farmers grow sugar beets, grains, potatoes, and other crops. Some land is used to raise animals for meat and dairy goods.

The Environment

The environment, or natural world, in Belgium is beautiful. The forests in this country include beech, oak, and spruce trees. To **protect** its natural beauty, Belgium has a number of

Flowers called bluebells give Hallerbos—a forest in Belgium—its nickname: the Blue Forest.

parks and reserves, which are spaces where animals and plants can be kept safe.

Belgium's coal mines closed in the 1990s. However, coal mines, trains, cars, and the growth of cities created air, land, and water pollution.

FACT!

Hydroelectric power plants in Belgium generate, or produce, electricity from rushing water.

Protecting the North Sea

The year 2018 was called the "Year of the North Sea." Beach cleanups were held in Belgium that year to protect the sea from plastic waste and other kinds of pollution.

To help the environment, Belgium is moving toward the use of only clean energy sources, or ways to get power.

Students in Belgium gathered in 2020 to call attention to the problem of pollution in the ocean.

Many Belgians fight pollution by riding bikes and walking instead of using cars. Having well-planned cycling paths makes this easier. Citizens also recycle to cut down on waste.

More than 98 percent of Belgium's population is urbanized, or lives in cities. As well as being one of the most urbanized countries in Europe, Belgium is also one of the most populated. Who are the more than 11 million people who live in Belgium?

More people live in Brussels than in any other Belgian city.

Belgians are often known by the region where they live. Flemings live in the northern region of Flanders. They speak Flemish and make up

FACT!

Differences between Walloon and Flemish Belgians have sometimes caused problems.

more than half of Belgians. Walloons live in the southern region of Wallonia. They make up one-third of the Belgian population and speak French. Another group of Belgians live in the

Belgians are all united under their country's flag, which is shown here.

Brussels-Capital region. This region officially has two languages: Flemish and French. The German language community of more than 77,000 people is in Eastern Belgium.

Different Backgrounds

Most people who live in Belgium are ethnically Belgian, which means their family roots are in Belgium. However, other Belgians come from French, Italian, Dutch, and Romanian backgrounds.

Lifestyle

Belgians living in cities are surrounded by stores and restaurants. They travel through and between cities by train, bus, bicycle, or car. Some Belgians live in apartments, but many others live in houses. In

Electric trams such as this one travel throughout Belgium.

some cases, these homes share a wall with the home next door.

Belgian children must attend school from ages 6 to 18. There are public and private schools, but students generally never have to pay for

FACT!

Most Belgians live in the northern two-thirds of the country.

The Belgian government tries to make sure everyone in the country has health care, housing, and fair wages. This is one of the reasons why Belgians are often said to have a high **quality** of life.

The Belgian constitution promises freedom of education for all.

school. Classes are taught in French, Flemish, or German depending on the school, though most students learn several languages. After students finish secondary school (known as high school in the United States), some go to universities, which are schools of higher learning. Other students go to schools that train them for jobs.

Religion

Around half of Belgians are Roman Catholics. The Roman Catholic religion, which is based on the teachings of Jesus Christ, has shaped Belgium's history. Catholic churches

Abbeys in Belgium, such as this one, are often very old.

and abbeys seem to be everywhere in the country. Some Belgians consider themselves Roman Catholics but don't attend church services, called masses, regularly.

Many Belgians don't practice any religion.

An abbey is where monks or nuns live.
They've made special promises to serve God.

St. Nicholas Day

Catholic holidays are big events in Belgium. St. Nicholas Day on December 6 is enjoyed with gifts and lots of chocolate!

They make up about 33 percent of the population. Another 9 percent are atheists, which means they don't believe in any kind of god. Muslims,

Shown here is a Muslim woman in Belgium.

who follow the teachings of Muhammad, make up about 5 percent of Belgians. This is a growing group in Belgium. A small number of Protestants practice in Belgium too. There's an even smaller Jewish population who live mainly in Brussels and Antwerp.

Language

Belgians speak three main languages. Flemish, which is a **version** of the Dutch language, is the most common. It's spoken by 60 percent of Belgians. Forty percent of Belgians

These Belgian students are learning the Dutch language in school.

speak French. German is spoken by around 1 percent of Belgians, especially in areas that had belonged to Germany before World War I. Around 10 percent of Belgians can speak both Flemish

FACT!

Brussels is home to the headquarters of the EU, and many European languages can be heard there!

22

Mixing French and Flemish

A small group of Belgians speak a special mixed language of French and Flemish. It's known by many different names, including Bruxellois and Marollian.

French and Flemish directions appear on signs in Brussels.

and French, and most of them live in or near Brussels.

For a long time, French was the main language of Belgium in government, business, and higher education. Flemings fought to have their language recognized. Today, Flemish, French, and German are all official languages of Belgium. In some large cities, street signs are written with French and Flemish side by side.

Arts and Festivals

Belgians have found fame through art, jazz music, fashion, film, books, comic strips, and more. Flanders has a great history of painting. The Flemish artist Jan van Eyck was a master of oil paints who

Shown here are Belgium's king and queen viewing art by Jan van Eyck.

lived in the 15th century. Other famous Belgian artists include Pieter Bruegel the Elder, Peter Paul Rubens, and René Magritte.

Music is a fun and much-loved part of Belgian

Belgian guitar player Django Reinhardt became one of the most famous European jazz musicians.

The Art of Comics

Belgians are proud of their comics. There's even a comic strip museum in Belgium! Characters such as Tintin and the Smurfs are Belgian creations.

Costumed dancers throw oranges during the Carnival of Binche.

culture. Jazz is popular for those who like the saxophone. The instrument was invented in Belgium by Adolphe Sax in the 1840s.

Nearly every city and village in Belgium has a special **festival**. Most are seasonal, historical, or religious. Carnivals are held around the country in the days before **Lent**. Most festivals include large parades, music, and fancy clothes called costumes.

Belgians like to have fun and enjoy life. Many head outdoors to hike in the Ardennes, travel along rivers and canals in boats, ride horses, or swim in the sea.

The beaches on Belgium's North Sea coast are popular places to visit.

The most popular sports in Belgium are cycling, soccer, tennis, judo, and hockey.

A number of large cycling races speed through Belgium. The Tour of Flanders takes place every spring over steep hills and cobblestone

Belgians like to take trips in the summer. They often visit the North Sea.

streets. Eddy Merckx, one of Belgium's favorite cyclists, won that race and many others in the 1960s and 1970s.

Shown here are cyclists taking part in the 2019 Tour of Flanders.

Soccer, or football as it's called in Belgium, is both played and watched. The Red Devils are the men's national team. Thousands of other teams and clubs play across the country.

History Happened Here

Some of Belgium's cities are more than 2,000 years old! Historic castles and abbeys can be visited in the cities and countryside.

Food

Most Belgians agree on which national foods are best, though they may like one city's version more than another's. Both Brussels and Liège brag about having the best waffles. Waffles are a snack often served on the street with powdered sugar, chocolate, fruit, or other toppings.

Belgium has many treats to offer visitors with a sweet tooth!

Belgian chocolate is eaten all around the world. Shoppers in Belgium can visit small, local

Brussels sprouts are named for the Belgian city of Brussels.

Say Cheese!

Belgium has a long history of making tasty cheese. More than 300 different kinds of cheese are made in this small country!

shops with fresh chocolates. There are many shapes and flavors to try! Belgians call the filled chocolates they enjoy so much pralines. Hot chocolate is also popular in Belgium.

French fries are known around the world, but Belgians believe they are the true inventors of fries. They're often served alongside mussels or in paper cones as a favorite street food.

A meal of fries and mussels is often called *moules frites*.

Glossary

canal   A man-made waterway.

festival   A time set aside to celebrate.

invade   To enter a country to take control by military force.

Lent   The period of 40 days before Easter Sunday that is considered a time of prayer and fasting for Catholics and some Protestants.

organization   A group that is formed for a specific purpose.

protect   To keep safe.

quality   How good or bad something is.

resource   Something that can be used.

revolution   The overthrowing of a ruler or government by force.

tourism   The business of drawing in tourists, or people traveling to visit another place.

version   A form of something that is different from others.

Find Out More

Books

Bowman, Chris. *Belgium*. Minnetonka, MN:
    Bellwether Media, Inc., 2020.

Cavell-Clarke, Steffi. *Belgium*. King's Lynn, UK:
    BookLife, 2017.

Website

National Geographic Kids: Belgium

*kids.nationalgeographic.com/explore/countries/
belgium/*

View pictures from famous sites, and learn new facts
about Belgium.

Video

The Carnival of Binche

www.youtube.com/watch?v=w8hXBbGmsxY

This video gives viewers a detailed look at the
Carnival of Binche in Belgium.

Index

About the Author

Rachael Morlock lives and writes in Western New York. She loves traveling to new places, both in person and through books.